THIS IS HOW FAR I'M WILLING TO GO--ANYBODY TRIES TO GET ME AWAY FROM THIS DESK OR CUT ME OFF--

--AND I'M BLOWING MY OWN BRAINS OUT.

MAKE SENSE.

SUFFERING AN APPARENT NERVOUS BREAKDOWN--

-- FORMER ANCHORWOMAN LONI HIROHITO HAS SEIZED CONTROL OF OUR BURBANK STUDIOS.

YOU SHUT UP. THIS IS MY SHOW.

BLAM BLAM

HUK HUK HUK

FOR GOD'S SAKE NOBODY INTERRUPT HER!

JUST YESTERDAY-- JUST YESTERDAY-- THINGS MADE SENSE...

THEY WERE WEIRD BUT THINGS MADE SENSE.

THEN TODAY I GET FIRED AND MY HUSBAND LEAVES ME AND THE PRESIDENT DIES AND SOME TWIT LIEUTENANT COLONEL TAKES OVER AND AMERICA IS HAVING A CIVIL WAR.

HUK HUK

JUST DOESN'T MAKE SENSE ... SOB ...

LONI--DON'T--

BLAMM

HISTORY AS IT HAPPENS--THIS IS AMERICA ON THE MOVE!

MAY 5, 2009: A TERRORIST FIREBOMB ROBS AMERICA OF THE MOST POPULAR PRESIDENT IN OUR COUNTRY'S HISTORY.

BUT ERWIN REXALL, CALLED BY MANY 'THE MAN WHO GAVE AMERICA ITS BALLS BACK'--

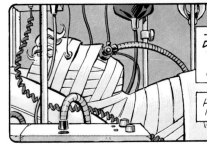

--DOES NOT DIE WITH THE REST OF HIS CABINET.

HIS BRAIN IS ALIVE.

THE VERY **BIRTH-PLACE** OF THE UNION --NEW ENGLAND--

--DEMANDS UNITED NATIONS REPRESENTATION AS AN **INDEPENDENT FEDERATION**.

MANHATTAN BOROUGH PRESIDENT **BELUGA** DECLARES **VICTORY** OVER **BROOKLYN**--

--ANNEXING IT AND FORMING THE **EAST COAST CAPITALIST DICTATORSHIP**.

BELUGA **DENIES** THE WIDESPREAD BELIEF THAT HE FACES AS MANY AS FORTY WARRING SEPERATIST MOVEMENTS WITHIN MANHATTAN.

THERE ARE SCATTERED REPORTS OF **SHELLING** ON THE BORDER OF THE **MEXICAN TERRITORY**--

-- AND THE SELF-PROCLAIMED **LONE STAR REPUBLIC**.

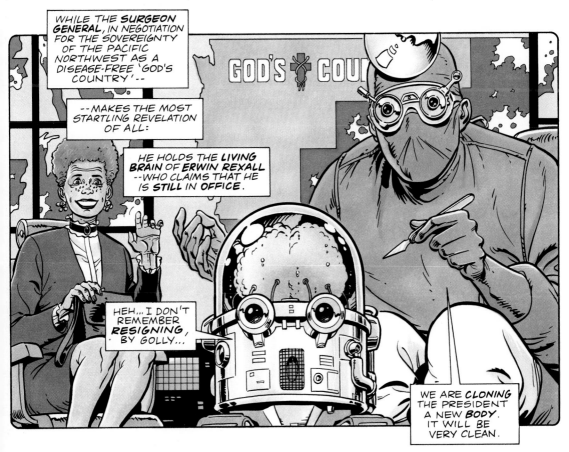

WHILE THE **SURGEON GENERAL**, IN NEGOTIATION FOR THE SOVEREIGNTY OF THE PACIFIC NORTHWEST AS A DISEASE-FREE 'GOD'S COUNTRY'--

--MAKES THE MOST STARTLING REVELATION OF ALL:

HE HOLDS THE **LIVING BRAIN** OF ERWIN REXALL --WHO CLAIMS THAT HE IS **STILL** IN OFFICE.

GOD'S COU[N]

HEH... I DON'T REMEMBER **RESIGNING**, BY GOLLY...

WE ARE **CLONING** THE PRESIDENT A NEW **BODY**. IT WILL BE VERY CLEAN.

IRONICALLY, IT WAS REXALL HIMSELF WHO DRAFTED THE 'NO HOLDS BARRED' AMENDMENT--

--COMMITTING **MILITARY FORCE** AGAINST ANY ENEMY WHO HOLDS AN AMERICAN CITIZEN **HOSTAGE** ...

I'VE GOT A WHOLE LOT OF WORK TO DO.

I'VE GOT TO SAVE THE *PRESIDENT*--SAVE A CREW OF *EIGHTY* ON A *SPACE CANNON*

--AND SAVE *RAGGYANN* AND THAT BIG *INDIAN* GUY.

RAGGYANN'S *PSYCHIC*...

SIDEKICK.

MARTHA MARTHA TALK-THINK.

WHAT'S YOUR *STATUS*? HAVE THEY PLUGGED YOU IN?

MOVE IT-- COME ON-- MOVE IT--

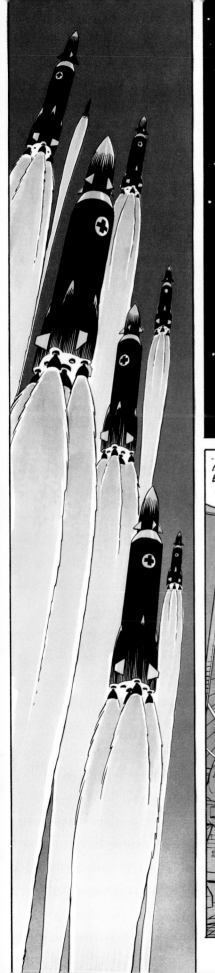

Repeat. This is not a drill. All hands to Battle Stations. Prepare to lay in defense grid.

WE'RE IN *TROUBLE*, COLONEL. WE'RE STILL *TEN* MINUTES FROM *DEPLOY-MENT*--

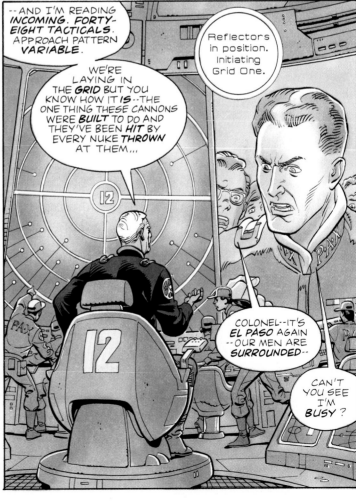

--AND I'M READING *INCOMING*. *FORTY-EIGHT TACTICALS*. APPROACH PATTERN *VARIABLE*.

WE'RE LAYING IN THE *GRID* BUT YOU KNOW HOW IT *IS*--THE ONE THING THESE CANNONS WERE *BUILT* TO DO AND THEY'VE BEEN *HIT* BY EVERY NUKE *THROWN* AT THEM...

Reflectors in position. Initiating Grid One.

COLONEL--IT'S *EL PASO* AGAIN --OUR MEN ARE *SURROUNDED*--

CAN'T YOU SEE I'M *BUSY*?

BOOM

BOOM

GOD'S COUNTRY:
The coalition government formed by the Surgeon General and leaders of the New Calvinist Initiative pledges to "lay waste to the impure" and create a smoke-free, drug-free paradise." Prohibited under penalty of death: "bad music, bad food, bad language, contraception, pornography, and adultery." 50,000 battle-hardened Health Enforcement Troops and Pacific Northwest nuclear missile silos provide a formidable military capability.

WONDERLAND:
The world's largest entertainment complex, it used to be the nation's playground. But funny animal robots are on the warpath demanding "cultural autonomy" and an "end to the enslavement of artificial intelligence." Rumors of mass murder and subjugation of humans remain unconfirmed. Should PAX assault Wonderland, a hostage crisis of unheard-of proportions is a likely scenario. Implementation of the "No holds Barred" Amendment could result in the death of millions.

REAL AMERICA:
Fat Boy Burger troops surround multimillion-acre cattlefields, breeding, slaughtering and selling to beef-hungry clients in flagrant defiance of the 94th Amendment. The outlaw fast food conglomerate is well-equipped to defend its territory: its million man army and formidable air force were almost a match for PAX in the Amazon War.

THE MEXICAN TERRITORY:
Still technically United States property, this overpopulated land openly trades with Real America and is Fat Boy's chief source of inexpensive labor. Satellite photos reveal hundreds of illegal cattle-fields, so many that analysts have stopped calling the territory "America's Ireland"; now it's "Burger Heaven." Anti-American sentiment is high, and Mexican-born PAX officers are joining the Fat Boy army in droves. An alliance between the two powers would present an unspeakable threat to the U.S. sovereignty over North America.

A NATION

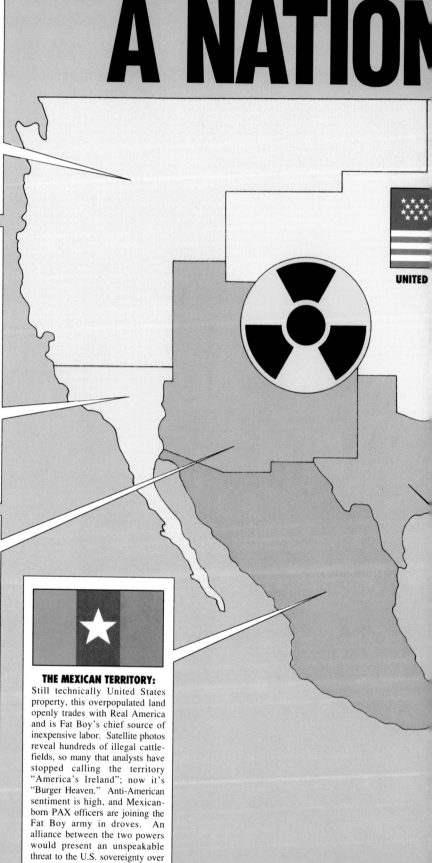

UNITED

DIVIDED

THE NEW ENGLAND FEDERATION OF STATES:

Militarily weak, this is the most pacifistic of the new governments, and the most likely to seek reunification with the U.S. Sticking point: the Federation seeks to repeal nearly every Constitutional Amendment passed since 1990. And those Green Mountain eggheads who engineered the schiz-out of the IRS Database in 2009 are bound to be up to more mischief than ever.

AMERICA

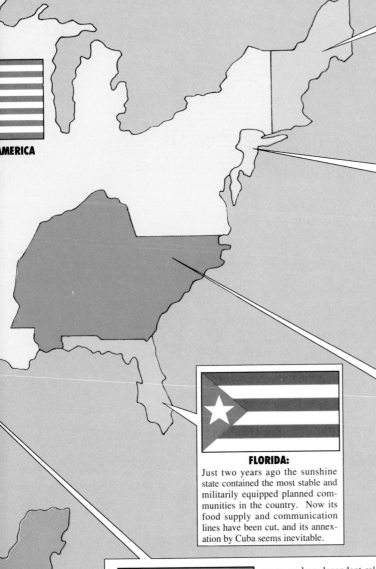

THE EAST COAST CAPITALIST DICTATORSHIP

Manhattan strongman Edward Beluga represents no major threat at present to U.S. security. Though strong in conventional forces, Beluga commands no nuclear, chemical or biological capability as yet. Besides, he has his hands full: his troops, weary from the year long Manhattan-Brooklyn War are now fighting block by block against the white gay racist Aryan Thrust, the Black Supremacy Front, and as many as fifty other separatist movements.

FLORIDA:

Just two years ago the sunshine state contained the most stable and militarily equipped planned communities in the country. Now its food supply and communication lines have been cut, and its annexation by Cuba seems inevitable.

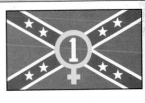

THE FIRST SEX CONFEDERACY:

Former First Lady Amanda Nissen, declaring that "everything wrong in the world has been caused by men," emerged as leader in the powerful Southeast Women's Movement, uniting its warring factions to overthrow the governments of the Old South. In her first address, she hit an encouraging note, assuring the U.S. that the Confederacy will seek diplomatic relationships and free trade. The South's abundant farmlands offer a crucial supply of food. Borders remain closed at present to male U.S. citizens. Nissen ordered bans on pornography, marriage, sexist remarks, and "negative role models" in entertainment. Missile silos in the area are abundant but in poor repair. However, a single orbiting laser cannon now answers directly to Nissen, discouraging invasion by PAX.

THE LONE STAR REPUBLIC:

Texas holds fast to its borders—and to its habits. With a platform of "Guns, beef, and beer" Dallas dentist Billy Bob Coolant established a government based on "community standards," rejecting the First, Fifth, and 94th Amendments out of hand. Their warm and co-dependant relationship with Fat Boy Burgers leaves little room for doubt whose side they would stand on if war breaks out between Fat Boy and PAX. Only Texan hatred of Fat Boy porn movies and continuing border skirmishes with the Mexican Territory prevent a full-fledged alliance. Texas commands a 300,000 man army and possesses first-strike nuclear capability on every city in the western hemisphere. The next American president will have to weigh carefully Texan displeasure with the U.S. Constitution as written.

ON THE WAY *SOUTH* I ASK THE BIG *INDIAN* WHAT HIS *NAME* IS.

HE SAYS IT'S *WASSERSTEIN*.

I TELL HIM THAT DOESN'T SOUND VERY *APACHE*.

HE *LAUGHS* AND SAYS *MY* NAME DOESN'T SOUND VERY *AFRICAN*.

Retros firing. Readying hydrofoil.

HAVEN'T SEEN THE *FOREST* SINCE THE *WAR*. THOUGHT I'D *NEVER* GET TO SEE IT AGAIN.

THE *REFORESTERS* ARE DOING A *GREAT* JOB. IT'S GOING TO BE AS BIG AS IT *EVER* WAS.

AND EVERY-BODY SAYS *NISSEN* WAS A *BAD* PRESIDENT.

HE WAS RIGHT ABOUT THE FOREST.

Distress signal engaged. Frequency 444.

WHAT THE *HELL...?*

OH, DEAR. OH MY WORD. I'LL GET A *COLD* AND YOU'LL GO ALL *RUSTY...*

NOW I'M SURE THOSE NICE BOYS THAT BUILT THIS MADE ME *WATER PROOF,* HONEY.

YOU'VE GOT TO LEARN TO *DEPEND* ON PEOPLE. THAT'S WHAT THEY'RE *THERE* FOR.

...I SAID, *ARE YOU CRAZY*? YOU'RE LETTING THEM *KNOW* WHERE WE ARE!

MARTHA NOT FLOP, TOMHAWK. NO *LUNCH BOX.*

BY NOW, *PAX* HAS THE SIGNAL AND THEY'VE PASSED IT ALONG TO MORETTI.

MY GUESS IS WE'VE GOT A FEW HOURS TILL HE GETS HERE.

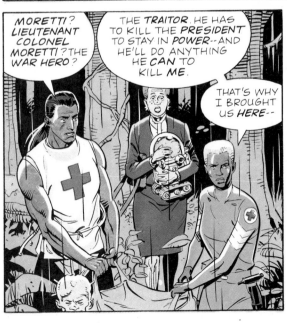

MORETTI? LIEUTENANT COLONEL MORETTI? THE WAR HERO?

THE *TRAITOR.* HE HAS TO KILL THE *PRESIDENT* TO STAY IN *POWER*--AND HE'LL DO ANYTHING HE *CAN* TO KILL *ME.*

THAT'S WHY I BROUGHT US *HERE*--

--THIS *FOREST* IS PROTECTED BY AN *EXECUTIVE ORDER.* MORETTI WON'T BE ABLE TO USE *BOMBS* OR A *LASER CANNON*--THE WAY HE DID ON YOUR *TRIBE.*

HE WAS JUST TRYING TO GET AT ME. I'M REALLY SORRY.

WE'LL CAMP HERE. WE'LL NEED A FIRE...

NOW LET'S SEE WHAT THE SURGEON GENERAL CALLS A FIRST AID KIT.

HOLY,...

YACHOO

CATCH MY DEATH OF COLD.

WE'LL JUST HAVE TO SNUGGLE ...HEH...

FIRST AID

OUR ODDS JUST GOT BETTER.

LET'S CATCH US SOME FROGS.

FROGS?

YOU'VE GOT TO BE CAREFUL NOT TO HURT THE FROGS.

THE NATIVES HERE WORSHIP THEM AND YOU'VE GOT TO RESPECT THAT SORT OF THING.

THEIR SKIN MAKES POISON.

THE NATIVES USE IT ON THEIR ARROWS.

Z

MY BET IS MORETTI WILL PUT TOGETHER A DEATH SQUAD-- MAYBE A DOZEN MEN. THE KIND WHO'LL KEEP THEIR MOUTHS SHUT.

HE'LL PROBABLY GET THEM FROM SQUAD FOUR...

SQUAD FOUR...? IS THAT PART OF THE PEACE FORCE?

Attention. This vehicle is at self-destruct alert. Detonation in three seconds pending voice identification.

OH, SHIT--

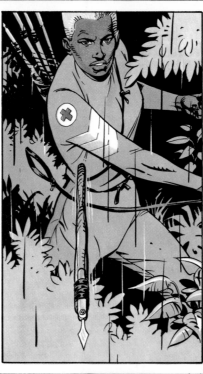

SIX.

WE'RE DOING **GREAT.**

BRAKK

BRAKK

SEVEN.

BRAKK

THKK

SEVEN. THAT LEAVES FIVE. AND MORETTI.

THERE--I GOT THE *SIGNAL* --REXALL IS A HALF MILE *NORTHEAST*-- LET'S *GO*--

NO. NOT YET. WE'VE GOT TO CONFIRM THE KILLS.

WE *HIT* THEM *BOTH*, MORETTI. LET THE *JUNGLE* DO THE REST.

WASHINGTON *CAN'T* BE LEFT *ALIVE*. THERE CAN'T BE ANY *DOUBT*.

YOU'RE *HUNG UP* ON THAT SNATCH, MORETTI. IT'S THROWING YOUR *JUDGEMENT* OFF--

--HEY...

ARE YOU CHALLENGING MY AUTHORITY?

NO, SIR. FOR THE RECORD, I AM NOT QUESTIONING YOUR AUTHORITY. WE WILL COMPLY WITH WHATEVER ORDER YOU CHOOSE TO GIVE.

...WE MOVE ON PRIMARY TARGET. REXALL. THEN A FINAL SWEEP OF THE AREA.

YES, SIR. WHATEVER YOU SAY.

LET'S MOVE!

YOU JUST HOLD ON. JUST HOLD ON. I'LL COME BACK FOR YOU.

SHOULDER'S NO GOOD. WON'T BE ABLE TO USE MY SLING.

NO. GUN'S NO GOOD.

HAVE TO USE THE RAIN.

IT'S SO LOUD IT'LL DROWN OUT ANYTHING QUIETER THAN A GUNSHOT.

THEY CALL IT THE *ROOF OF THE WORLD.*

THAT'S WHAT THE NATIVES CALL IT.

THEY THINK THE FOREST IS THE WHOLE WORLD AND FOR THEM IT IS.

FIVE LEFT.

AND MORETTI.

RAIN'S SO LOUD.

I HAVE A CHANCE.

BRAKK

P·A·X

BRAKABRAKABR

KRAKK

CHIK

MORETTI-- NO -- I'VE GOT HER--

CHKCHAKK

KRAKKK

COLONEL MORETTI.
YOU ARE UNDER ARREST.

DETAINED
WITHOUT BAIL--
FACING CHARGES
OF *TREASON*
INCLUDING THE
BRUTAL *MURDER*
OF THE *FIRST
LADY*--

--AND WITH
THE ATTEMPTED
ASSASSINATION OF
PRESIDENT REXALL.

ON THE EVE OF A
SPECIAL ELECTION,
REXALL IS SHOWN
LEADING IN EVERY
POLL NATIONWIDE...

LIEUTENANT **WASHINGTON** TO SEE YOU, COLONEL.

LIEUTENANT. SHE MADE LIEUTENANT. I SHOULD'VE KNOWN. SEND HER ON IN. WHY THE HELL NOT.

YOU KNOW WHAT KIND OF PLACE I GREW UP IN, COLONEL. A LOT OF PEOPLE I KNEW ENDED UP IN PRISON, JUST LIKE YOU.

ONE REAL GOOD FRIEND I HAD WHEN I WAS A **KID**, HE GOT **FRAMED** FOR **MURDER**. ENDED UP FACING THE **DEATH PENALTY**.

THEY WERE GOING TO USE AN ANTIQUE **ELECTRIC CHAIR** ON HIM, NOT A **FIRING SQUAD** LIKE THE ONE YOU'RE FACING.

I VISITED HIM IN HIS CELL. HE ASKED ME FOR MY **BELT** AND I GAVE IT TO HIM.

LIKE I SAID, I WAS JUST A **KID**. I DIDN'T KNOW WHY HE WANTED IT UNTIL THE NEXT **MORNING**.

I GUESS THE WAITING WAS THE WORST OF IT FOR HIM.

DON'T GO. I DON'T WANT TO BE ALONE WHEN I DO IT.

YES, SIR.